# How to Care for Your Monster

Written and illustrated by NORMAN BRIDWELL

## SCHOLASTIC INC.

New York   Toronto   London   Auckland   Sydney

*To Eddie Stalling*

ISBN 0-590-40782-1

Copyright © 1970, 1988 by Norman Bridwell.
All rights reserved. Published by Scholastic Inc.
Art direction by Diana Hrisinko.
Text design by Emmeline Hsi.

12 11 10 9 8 7 6 5 4 3          0 1 2 3/9

Printed in the U.S.A.          11

First Scholastic printing, February 1988

# How to Care for Your Monster

So you want to own a monster? Many people do these days. You can bring a monster into your home. It's just a matter of finding one you like.

This book will tell you how to get your monster and how to keep him healthy and happy.

If you are lucky enough to live in a town that has a Monster Store, getting a monster should be easy. Just show Dad the ad and ask him for some money.

Thank him and run — before he asks questions.

MONSTER?

Most Monster Stores open at midnight, so you may
want to take a friend along.

If new monsters are too expensive, buy a used monster. Check him carefully. Used monsters may be slightly damaged.

Some have been thrown over cliffs or burned a little in old windmills by angry owners or hard-to-please villagers.

If you can't buy a new or used monster, perhaps you can have one made to order.

The Frankenstein monster is put together in a way I would rather not go into. Making one is not a do-it-yourself project. I suggest that you ask your friendly neighborhood Mad Doctor for help. He

will enjoy picking up the pieces and putting them together. And he probably won't charge *you* — just the monster.

Your friendly neighborhood Mad Doctor may already have a monster hidden somewhere in his office. Look around. If you find him and he likes you, he may follow you home. The monster, not the doctor.

When you get your monster home, make him comfortable. Put him in a dark corner in the cellar. The darker the better — he's used to caves and old rotting windmills.

He will feel better the first night if you rattle a chain and shriek a little.

Frankenstein monsters usually don't eat. But they do need electricity now and then to keep them going. You remember that Dr. Frankenstein brought his monster to life with a good jolt of lightning. If yours seems sluggish and dull, hand him a

metal pole and send him out to play in a thunderstorm — ALONE! He'll love it.

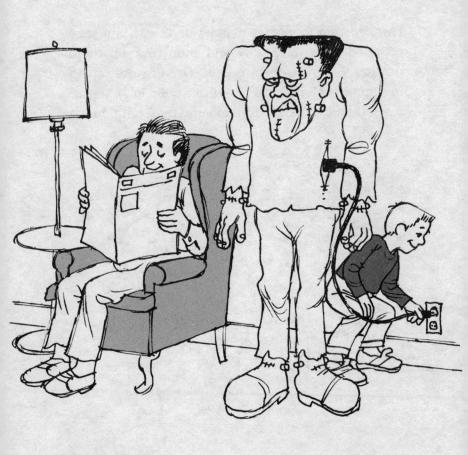

I don't need to tell you that plugging him into the house electricity can be dangerous.

It can cause trouble.

Sometimes, after a really good thunderstorm, your monster may be overcharged. Help him get rid of his excess energy. Let him run the vacuum cleaner — and other things.

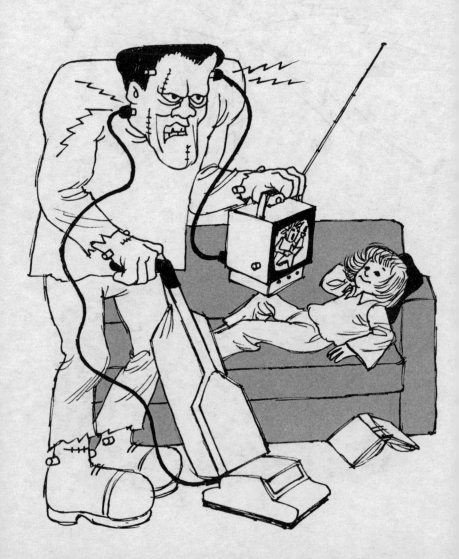

Another good way to work off his extra energy is to take him for a walk. He will not like to go out in the sunlight. Understand his problem. Make it pleasant for him.

If he wants to explore a few dark cellars or man-holes, let him.

A little curiosity never hurt anyone.

Your Frankenstein monster enjoys meeting people. Introduce him to your friends. They will get a real charge out of him.

Frankenstein monsters are the nicest kind of monster because they look like monsters *all* the time. Give your monster pride in his appearance. Polish his neck and wrist bolts, and sew up any loose stitches.

If you can't sew, maybe Mom will help. Good luck.

To keep his skin a nice smooth green, try using your big sister's green eye shadow.

Halloween is a big night in any monster's life. Help yours to make the most of it. Take him trick or treating. Here's the trick —

Now here's the treat (Frankenstein monsters have a real sense of fun.).

Share your activities with your monster. After all, he is almost like one of the family. In fact, he's probably better than some of the family. He will like to watch horrible, mean, nasty shows on television. Let him watch the news.

Now we move on to another popular monster.

# Dig Up a Friend—A Mummy

If your family is always telling you to turn down the record player and not to shout, giggle, or slam doors, then a mummy is the monster for you. He makes very little noise...

...except at night. Then your mummy will go thump-thump across the attic floor, right over the family's heads. Well, that will show them what noise really is.

Where to find your mummy:

If your local Monster Store doesn't stock mummy-monsters, you have a problem. Unless someone in your family has stolen a Mummy's Hand. In that case, the mummy will find *you*. But don't count on it. Maybe you can get acquainted with a mummy in your local museum.

You might also try looking through the museum's trash barrels. Perhaps an old, used mummy is being thrown away.

Or maybe you have a friend who is planning to visit
Egypt soon. Ask him to pick up a mummy for you.

Then you can be sure of having a genuine Egyptian
mummy in the best of health.

Mummies don't eat. But they enjoy spices, and they need some balsam and aromatic gums now and then to keep them from crumbling.

Save your old Christmas trees for the balsam. As for aromatic gums, try Spearmint and Juicy Fruit.

Keep the mummy dry. No one likes a soggy mummy. The outer wrappings can be dusty but not dirty. If your mummy gets dirty, take off the outside wrappings. Don't unwrap him too far!

Let your little brother or sister play with him. Mummies like to bury things in the sandbox. They also like to play with blocks. Mummies are good at building pyramids.

Mummies don't laugh or smile, but most of them are good-natured. This is surprising when you know what they went through to become mummies.

Mummies like to have fun, too. So when a salesman comes to your door and asks to see your "mummy," let him.

Once in a while, after a mummy comes to live in your house, you will start having bad luck. What you have is The Mummy's Curse. Don't blame your mummy. If someone woke you up from a 2,000 years' sleep, you'd be grouchy, too.

# Vampires—From Bat to Worse

Vampire fans find it a real challenge to have a vampire around the house. If you want to have a vampire without going to the Monster Store, try this.

Just before dawn, when bats fly back to their caves, go out into the yard. Take a cap with you. When a bat flies by, shout, "Bat, bat, fly into my hat." Throw the cap up in the air. If a bat flies into it, he will fall to the ground. Pop him into a cage and go back to bed. When the sun comes up, look in the cage.

Maybe you will have a bat.

Or you may have a real vampire.

If you do, introduce yourself and ask him courteously if he is looking for a new home. He probably is. Vampires change owners often.

Vampires are very dignified and polite. But they have rather peculiar habits of eating and sleeping.

So don't bother to fix up the guest room. Your vampire will be happier in a damp corner of the cellar, with his own special bed to lie in when he goes to ___ dawn.

This brings us to the fact that your vampire will want to sleep all day and play all night. Nighttime is the right time for him to play. Vampires enjoy a game of night baseball...

...as long as they are at bat. You know how they are about bats.

They also enjoy playing bat-minton.

Now we come to the biggest problem a vampire fan must face. Vampires don't eat the foods we do — they crave a special liquid diet.

So a vampire-owner needs to have a large and understanding family and a lot of very good friends who will help out at feeding time. One person can't do it all alone.

But if your vampire should enjoy too many mid-night snacks at your expense, just rub garlic on your neck. He hates garlic. It will keep him away. It will also keep away Mom, Dad, brothers, sisters, friends, the dog, etc.

Vampires hate other things. Serve your vampire hot cross buns, and he will leave the table.

Vampires do not cast reflections in mirrors. They hate mirrors for that reason.

They are very conceited about their appearance, however, so you will have to keep your vampire looking neat. In that case you may prefer a shaggier monster....

# Werewolves
## —Hair Today, Gone Tomorrow

If you want a werewolf, you will have to face the fact that you will have a part-time monster. Most of the month a werewolf will look like you or me. Well, me, anyway. But when the moon is full he will be a real monster and well worth the wait.

Werewolves like full moons, wolfsbane, and boys and girls. Tell your friends to lock up their little brothers when the moon is full. That is the best time to catch a werewolf — when the moon is full. Take a handful of wolfsbane out to the woods and wait. Wolfsbane is the werewolves' version of catnip. It drives them wild.

If you are lucky, a werewolf will soon come out of the woods to nibble the wolfsbane and howl at the moon. Don't try to reason with him. Just slap a big cage over him. You can explain things later when the moon has changed.

If you can talk him into staying, you and your friends will find that he is a fun monster.

Werewolves are not fussy about their appearance. The worse they look the better. They usually come back from moonlight romps with their clothes all soiled with mud and grass stains and, uh, well... other things.

While the moon is full it is wise to keep your werewolf well-fed with raw meat and wolfsbane. Otherwise he may stop by the neighbors for a little snack.

If he acts sluggish and out of sorts, take him to the doctor or to a veterinarian. Which one you take him to depends on the moon. Don't delay. It could be distemper...

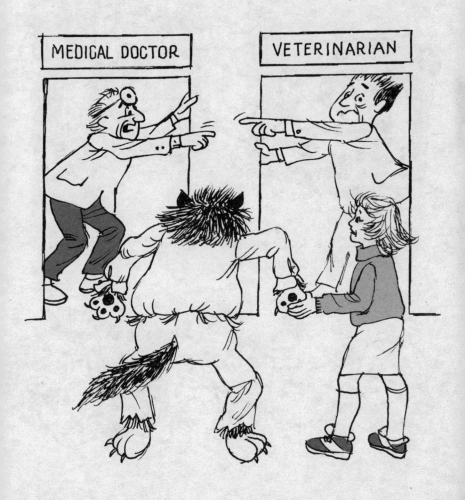

...or it could be someone he ate. Count your friends.

Don't blame your monster. After all, you wanted a werewolf, and you got it.

# How to Have a Monster Show
## —Howl, Howl, the Gang's All Hair

When you and your friends all have monsters, it will be fun for the owners to have a monster show. Give prizes for the best ones. Why should the dog and horse lovers have all the fun?

The show must be held on a night when the moon is full, so that *all* the monsters will be monsters. Choose a place where they will be at their best. Any haunted house or deserted graveyard will do.

You will need judges. There must be *someone* you know who is used to dealing with monsters. How about your teacher?

Here are some tips to the judges on what to look for in monsters before awarding the prizes.

Frankenstein monsters should be judged for ugliness, size, surliness, and charm. The shine of their wrist and neck bolts as well as the electrodes on

AAAARRRRGGGH !

**A Winner**

their heads will be considered. So will the quality of their seam stitching. The best shriek will count points.

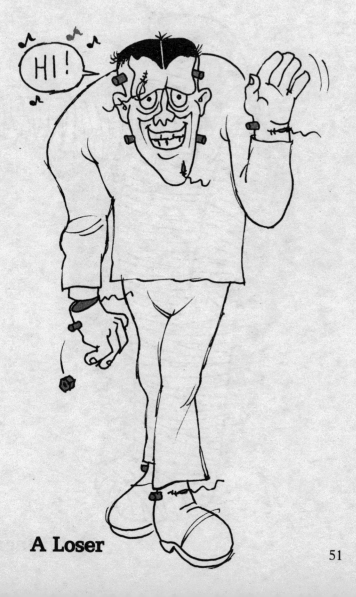

**A Loser**

Mummies get points for best wrapping, worst aroma, and heaviest feet. Make sure your mummy

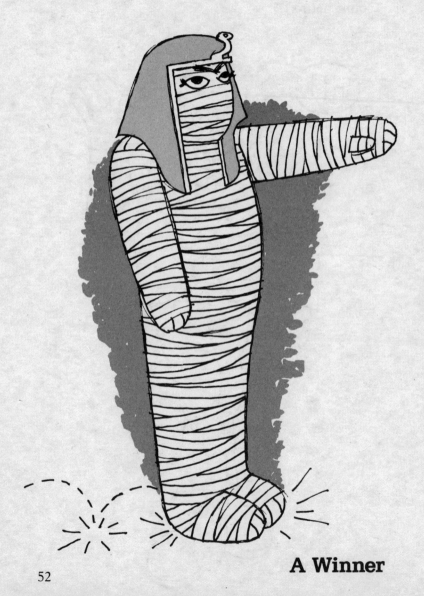

**A Winner**

thumps slowly and loudly across the stage. No tap
dancing, please.

**A Loser**

Vampires should look especially neat and dapper. Capes must be neatly pressed but with just a hint of graveyard mold. Hair should be shiny and slicked down.

**A Winner**

Teeth must be sharp and bite must be neat. Only two punctures per bite, please. Judges should look for an evil glare in the eyes.

## A Loser

The werewolf will be judged for the length and coarseness of his hair and the size and sharpness of his claws. His howl will be judged. The louder

**A Winner**

the better. His ability to recognize the moon will also be considered. If he howls at a light bulb you might as well take him home right away.

**A Loser**

As for the prizes, give the mummies ribbons. They love ribbons.

Never give a silver medal to a vampire. Vampires are terrified of silver for some reason. Toss a vampire an old dime sometime and see what happens.

If a Frankenstein monster wins a prize, give him something he can use. Give him a trip to the power plant.

Werewolves are always thinking of their stomachs. Give them a prize they can eat. Give them the judge.

Sometimes monsters are better to give than to receive. For that brother or sister or friend who is very special to you, choose a gift that will bring new surprises each day throughout the year, and be a reminder of you. Give a monster. He won't know how to thank you.

There, that's all you need to know about monsters. Now go out and catch one. Don't be the last in your neighborhood to have a monster.